Cha Cha's Diary

Dog Tales

Eileen Geeson

Dedication

To Standard Poodles everywhere but especially to Jane, Sarah, Candy, Samantha, Vicky, Elvis, Barry, Denim, Rainbow, Tory, Beryl, Goldie, Penny, Velvet, Remi, Treasle and not forgetting Katie and Cha Cha - with ever my love.

The author

Eileen Geeson has been actively involved with dogs for over thirty years, having close experience with many breeds, but her first love has always been the Poodle. She has prepared and handled many breeds for their owners for the show ring. Taking show ring training classes she is in regular contact with most breeds and talks to breeders and groomers on a daily basis, as well as always being available to help out pet dog owners. Actively involved in Showing Poodles since 1964, she has bred English, Finnish, Swedish and International Champions. Eileen is a Championship Show judge with a world record of Standard Poodle entries to her credit. She has been on the committee of The Standard Poodle Club for twenty years, serving five years as Vice-Chairman. Eileen is the author of *The Complete Standard Poodle* (Ringpress), which is enjoying worldwide success, as well as contributing the 'Looking Good' section to *The Ultimate Puppy* (Ringpress). She is the author of *The Ultimate Book Of Dog Grooming* (Ringpress), to be released in Spring 2001. She is a contributing writer to the Dog Papers and pet dog publications and writes Romance and Crime novels.

Published by Kingdom Books

© 2001 Eileen Geeson.

Photos courtesy of Steph Holbrook

Cha Cha says...

Hello. My name is Cha Cha. I am a white female Standard Poodle. My Dad, Roy, who is married to my Mum, Eileen, says that it is my good breeding that gives me such a mystified air of pomp and grandeur. Mum says that I don't look so aristocratic when I have been chasing rabbits through a dyke but she supposed all young aristocrats have an impish streak. Impish? I don't know what she means...

When Velvet's litter of five were born, Mum decided to keep me because she says she couldn't resist the loving look in my eyes. Well, she's always loved me to bits, ever since I can first remember, so what else could I do but love her. Dad says she spoils me but she says he's just as bad!

I don't know what it was that first inspired me to write a diary. I think Mum had an extra one for Christmas and it was lying around looking abandoned. I remember picking it up one day and chewing idly at the hard edges of the colourful pageant jacket. Mum took it off me and turned it over in her hands, contemplating its near destruction. Then she said something like "If you're that keen on the diary Cha Cha, you can have it!"

Well I don't seem to have stopped writing since. Perhaps you would care to have a peep inside....

A Degree of Intelligence

The Reader's Digest came in the post. Mum sorted it from the other mail and flicked through it with idle curiosity. Suddenly her attention was caught. She said to Dad, as he sat at the kitchen table nibbling hot buttered toast and sipping steaming tea, "Look at this! *Test Your Dog's Intelligence - he may be smarter than you think. Canine genius; very smart; average; generally thick; blissfully ignorant!*"

Dad laughed. "Let's have a look." Mum handed him the booklet and he read out loud: "*Blessed with a well-developed brain, superb physical senses and a very strong ability and willingness to learn, the dog has a high level of intelligence...*"

"We know all that," Mum commented. "We also know they can think for themselves - especially if they are Standard Poodles - and they have a brilliant memory. Look at Daisy. We hadn't seen her since she was nine weeks old and when she came in last week - having not been here for a whole year - she went straight over to sniff, with great application, the corner of the kitchen where the whelping box that she had been born in had stood."

Dad nodded his head, an expression of wonder in his dark brown eyes. "Yes. Incredible. She knew where she had been born! And what about Cha Cha the other day, when she went to your sister, Sylvia's."

"I know!" Mum exclaimed with awe, looking at me with as though some phenomenon had taken place. "She knew precisely where Sylvia had put that teddy-bear of the children's and immediately went to that spot."

"Makes these questions seem stupid," Dad said, getting back to the article.

"Read all the questions out," Mum suggested. "Let's see how our lot do for cleverness."

Dad nodded. "*Question number one - With your dog watching, make as if to reach for a snack and pretend to eat it.*
Your dog:
a) Watches you intently as if you are actually eating.
b) Investigates the spot from which you took the 'food' to see if anything is there.
c) Couldn't be less interested.
d) Seems to realise you're just pretending."

Mum said "We'll try it." She went to the cupboard, pulled out a tin of biscuits and took off the lid - which activated an interesting observation from Goldie, Tory and Velvet. (I stood on the side watching). Penny wasn't much interested after a quick glance at the tin from a distance. Of course, I knew what she was thinking. Since when did they share the contents from that particular tin with visitors, let alone us!

Dad pretended to take a biscuit from the proffered tin and Mum did likewise. Well, you should have seen the expression on Goldie's face! She obviously thought the dear pair had finally lost their marbles. Tory glanced at me and commented in her silent way - they have gone nuts! Are they mad? I mean fancy eating an imaginary biscuit?

Velvet watched the tin, waiting for something real to happen - or wishing! She'll be lucky, as if a biscuit will pop out of the tin and fall straight into her mouth! Penny stretched and wandered up, her nose in the air like a top-lofty princess, she made a snort, saying "We never get anything from that blue tin - now, if it were the red one!" She poked Mum with her damp nose and lifted her face in the air - staring up at the cupboard where our tit-bit biscuit tin was kept.

"D," Mum said. "This lot know we are pretending. They are not daft."

"Top score," Dad said with little surprise. "Next question...
Does your dog appear to remember people, such as relatives who only visit occasionally?
a) No.
b) Yes, especially if they were friendly to your dog on the last visit.
c) Sometimes.
d) No, but it will act as if it remembers if they offer it some food."

There was a quick answer to that. "Yes," Mum said, "Daisy remembered us and we hadn't seen her for a year!"

"Remarkable that," Dad said. "Now that's good memory! Most of these questions actually relate to memory and how much training the dog has had - like if you have taught it to sit at the kerb before crossing the road etc."

"Nobody taught Cha Cha to catch rabbits!"

"That's the instinct of survival."

"And nobody taught her to be so gentle and loving towards severely handicapped people."

"That's inheritance too, bestowed upon her by her compassionate grandmother."

"She has got an uncanny sense of understanding any given situation, and responding to it." Mum looked at me with tenderness in her green eyes.

"I know. Look at her now. The way she is looking from you to me. That expression! The looks she is giving us makes you wonder if she isn't sitting there making up her own twenty questions on testing your owner's intelligence."

Mum laughed. "Why don't we ask her?"

I glanced at them and twitched my nose in a secret smile. *Human genius? Very smart? Average?* I rested my head against Mum's knee. She bent down and put her arms around me to kiss my face. I murmured contentedly to the others "*Blissfully ignorant*, I think, girls." They agreed.

Signing off for now
Cha Cha

A Day at Skegness

Dad's got a new car! He's longing to take it for a spin so we're off to visit Auntie Jeanne in Skegness. Auntie Dot - our friend and sitter - and her dog (my sister, Katie) are coming with us for a ride. Eilene and Preston (E&P from up the road) are coming to see to the girls we have to leave at home. Mum explains that as Katie and me are still so young we need to get about and meet people, to be socialised. I'm not arguing. I love going on trips.

Dad puts a clean blanket on the back seat of his shiny new car and Katie and me jostle for prime position nearest Dot's lap. Eventually Mum gets exasperated with our pushing and shoving and suggests Dot sits in the middle of the seat with one of us either side. That settles the problem; Katie and I get half a lap each. We settle down

and go to sleep until Dad decides to start whistling and Katie jumps on his head, reaching round the head restraint to lick his ears. He mumbles and Mum suggests that instead of whistling he switches on the radio instead.

Presently we arrive at Auntie Jeanne's. As the car turns in, tyres crunching over gravel, Katie and I stand up to stare with unexpected glee at the sight before our eyes. Hordes of cars, and the field beside Jeanne's bungalow amass with people, dogs and brightly coloured obstacles. What's all this?

"Jeanne never said she had the Agility Club here this morning," Mum said. Dad asked if it mattered and she shook her head, looking quite pleased. "It'll be interesting, I'm sure." Dot was leaning forward in her seat, her lips parted in a wide smile, her eyes glowing. "I've never seen dogs doing agility; they jump hurdles and things, don't they? Like the horses do."

Katie and me were in ecstasy because whatever was going on looked like great fun. We had our leads put on and we all made our way over to the field gate. Auntie Jeanne, in her green Wellington boots, black cords and bright check shirt, opened the gate. "Come in. We are having a training day." She dismissed Dad's concern about our

diverting the working dogs' attention. Katie and me, as if we would! "These dogs won't be bothered by your two; they are far too well trained!" Jeanne boasted.

Well, I must say their activity did look rather good sport. German Shepherd Dogs (GSDs), large and colourfully marked, thick coats and panting tongues, ran up great leaning fences and down the other side. Border Collies (BCs) with their striking black/white flashes darted through a long collapsible tunnel, and a couple of rather wise, nicely turned out Standard Poodles were jumping through a tyre that was suspended in the air amid a wooden frame.

One of the SPs was our cousin, Jet. Unable to concentrate once he had seen us, Jet rushed over to say hello. Katie was immediately besotted and, I could see from the expression on her face, in show-off mood. Jeanne suggested to Mum that she let Katie and me off our leads to investigate. Mum looked hesitant for some reason but Jeanne managed to convince her that we would be no trouble, and we were free.

Jet sniffed Katie and ran off, expecting her to follow him, but I could see her eyes wandering. She always was a flirt. I followed him instead and he showed off by jumping over a hurdle. I took it after him. I'd done this at home with Mum. I thought Katie would follow once she saw what fun it was to jump but her mind was elsewhere. She had taken a fancy to a Border Collie, sniffed it, wagged her tail, flashed her eyes and fluttered her long eyelashes and, the next thing - the pair had taken off!

Katie was after a hare, at least, that was what I thought to begin with, the speed with which she was covering the ground. But no, she was merely showing off her physical fitness. The BC chased. Katie did a mid-air turn over the BC's back; it turned and then she was chasing him.

"Come! Down! Stay!" voices shouted from all directions. Did they expect Katie to take notice? They must be joking!

The BC was now in high spirits and had it's ears closed. Dot tried, without success, to catch Katie as she whooshed past. Another young BC decided this looked fun and tried to round them up. I wasn't having that. I intercepted it as it came through the middle of the A frame. It was a bit quick so I had to take off after it, suddenly realising that a GSD was on my tail. Well, I'd show him! I am faster than Katie and cut corners with greater balance. Another GSD thought this was a bit much and tried to block my way. I cleared him with no trouble and laughed at the look of surprise on his black-masked face. Trouble was, in doing this I was suddenly faced with one of those spread jumps - like you see on the Horse of The Year Show, only smaller. I cleared that; four, or was it six, dogs followed in my wake. I saw an opening and made for it. Darkness! Then, in a flash, out of this dark tunnel into daylight again.

Stealing a quick glance I saw Katie was behind me now; the BC, or was it three black and white flashes, came next, then two GSDs and Jet barking up the rear. I darted in and out of the trees and headed for a space. My mistake came when I ran through Mum's legs. She was knocked off-balance and she and I were on the ground in a tumble. Surprisingly she looked highly amused. Jeanne and Dot were laughing. Being Poodle owners they had to have a good sense of humour. Dad had disappeared, it was mentioned later, in sheer embarrassment. Several other people stood glaring, fists in the air, thunderous sounds exploding from their lips.

Katie and Jet came to enquire about the accident and Katie's new friend, the BC, hovered with a lovesick expression at Katie's side. Next thing they were having a tumble in the long grass. It was only when the BC stopped for a good scratch that they were captured and placed under control. Katie responded by having a scratch too.

We were led into Jeanne's kitchen where we happily flopped on the cold tiled floor for a snooze. Mum said something about doing Agility with me when I got older and my bones were set. Wiping her sweat-drenched brow Dot fell into a chair. Jeanne put the kettle on.

It was a good day, a day to remember. And when we got home, had dinner and settled down beside Mum and Dad's bed that night, I told the others about it. They nodded and I got the bit about "in our youth". You know the sort of thing. Goldie, of course, boasted. She had won prizes in Agility! Goldie is good at most things, especially taking up most of Dad's pillow as soon as he vacates the bed in the morning.

Soon I was asleep but not for long. Ouch... It felt like something bit me! Ouch. There it goes again. I nibble. I'm itching like mad and need a jolly good scratch. And another....and another....

Mum's awake, grumbling about the bed rocking. Dad moans about the noise as my foot bashes against the floor when I scratch. "Has that damn dog got fleas or something?"

"She only had a bath yesterday!"

"Well I reckon she's picked some up at Jeanne's."

"That Border Collie was doing rather a lot of scratching."

Scratch, scratch, the urge is uncontrollable. Mum gets out of bed mumbling about my losing coat. She lays me on my side and runs a hand over my tummy. She gasps! Then she is squeezing little black things as they crawl through my coat, trying to get away from her hands.

Mum's expression is one of utter despair. Without further ado she

whips me downstairs and starts grooming every inch of my coat with some dreadful smelling spray. Half an hour later we return to the bedroom and, still grumbling, Mum climbs into bed.

Velvet has started to chew at her leg. Penny decides she wants to scratch now. Goldie, who I always sleep close to, is banging against the bed with a vengeance. I saw a little black thing jump off her and onto Tory. Then Beryl started. Bite, bite, scratch, scratch.

"Heavens!" Mum exclaims as she leapt out of bed, tipping Dad out in her panic. "Get up." She wiped the bed clean of duvet and sheet in one fell swoop and sped down the stairs, calling us in her wake. Frantically she began to stuff the covers and things in the washing machine while looking positively on the verge of a nervous breakdown. Then she rushed like a demented dog back up the stairs clutching a bright yellow can in her hand. Presently Dad came down sneezing. He grumbled when Mum finally returned. "Couldn't you have waited until the morning?"

Mum retorted in a flash. "Don't blame me for the lack of sleep. If you hadn't been so keen to take your new car...."

He didn't wait for her to finish. "My car!" He grabbed the big yellow can and disappeared out to the garage.

Mum said, as she put the kettle on, "I suppose one day we will laugh about this."

Signing off for now
Cha Cha

Gardening

Had a bath first thing and Mum looked right pleased with herself as she stood surveying her hard work in transforming my rather off-white coat into a sparkling picture of pure white. Mum then got into some clean jeans and a bright top, collected her handbag and the car keys, told the others we wouldn't be long, and we left for Holbeach.

As soon as we turned left at the roundabout I knew where we

were going and I couldn't resist standing up on the back seat, peering out the window expectantly, with tail wagging from side to side. Soon enough Mum drew the car to a halt outside Auntie Dot's bungalow. Katie, my sister, came out of the door, speeding up to the car like a greyhound after a hare. Dot tottered up the drive after her and before long we were off again. Soon we arrived at the magnificent Bay Tree

Garden Centre. Mum had a quick chat with the owner, Reinhardt, about Katie and me accompanying her and Dot around while they searched for plants. Being a dog lover he was quite happy about it.

What was needed apparently were some shrubs that would grow through the Winter and be ready to cheer up the Spring and early Summer. Katie and I were put on leads and the search began. Dot wanted bright colours and it took quite a while to pick the right plants because there were so many to choose from.

Bay Tree Garden Centre is an immense place, with everything imaginable to cater for all the needs of keen gardeners or those with just an idle interest. There is a large pet section and a huge indoor children's adventure play area. It would have been good to be let loose but still Katie and I quite enjoyed our rather sedate ramble through the aisles and aisles of trees, shrubs, conifers and plants. It took a good hour to get halfway round. Eventually Mum and I went to get a trolley while Dot sat resting on a wall. When we returned Dot and Mum piled boxes and trays of little plants into it. Mum also treated herself to a nest of rather sterling looking earthenware pots for the patio. On the way home Mum and Dot talked enthusiastically about the wonderful splash of Spring colour the wallflowers would make to cheer up Dot's view from her sitting room in the early Spring. And the pansies and begonias would look lovely along the length of the garden path.

Arriving back at the bungalow, Mum and Dot struggled up the path to the back garden with all the trays of plants. Katie and I followed. We had a game with an old rubber boot while Mum and Dot went into the shed to retrieve a trowel, small garden fork and a watering can.

After our game in the sunshine Katie and I had a long drink from the fountain, Katie with her feet standing in the water of the fishpond while Dot wasn't looking. I climbed onto the swinging hammock for a snooze while Katie suddenly took an interest in the gardening proceedings. She sat as upright as a statue watching, with what I can only describe as serious fascination, as Mum and Dot bent and squatted, busily making little indents in the earth and pushing the plants we had just bought back from the garden centre into them. It was a very time-consuming process. In fact, it was at least two hours later that Mum stretched, pushing her hands into the small of her back, groaning, and Dot staggered and panted as she got into an upright position. Standing back to survey their efforts they looked well pleased. There was now a bed of wallflowers and what seemed like hundreds of tiny pansy and begonia plants edging the border of the path from the pond to the back patio window.

Mum and Dot expressed words of great satisfaction and Katie glanced up at them with a curious grin. They called us and we all went into the kitchen. Dot put the kettle on, after handing Mum some milk from the refrigerator, which she poured into two small bowls, placing down one each for Katie and me.

It was lovely. I decided to lie on my belly, dish between paws and lap slowly, savouring every tongue full. Katie took a lap or two then hesitated. I could see something was bothering her. Her mind was preoccupied. But she wouldn't let on what it was. After a second go at the creamy milk she left it and rushed outside.

Mum and Dot sat at the kitchen table sipping hot tea from bone-china cups while discussing the antics of Kissy, Mum's friend Stella's, seven year old Standard Poodle who she had just homed. They were aahing and having the odd giggle. Presently Mum sighed and said we ought to be going. We were taking Katie back with us because Dot was going away for two days on one of her coach trips. Mum glanced at me and smiled. I was ready.

"Where's Katie?"

"She must have gone out into the garden again," Dot said. She called Katie.

Katie didn't come immediately and Dot was about to go out to see

why when her fluffy blue body finally rushed in through the back door. Grinning from ear to ear, she looked a picture of puppyish innocence.

"Oh dear!" exclaimed Dot. "I know that look!"

Mum twisted her mouth and bit on her lower lip. "Katie's got muddy feet!"

Katie, well satisfied, ran back outside with a spring in her step and a high wagging tail. Mum, Dot and I followed.

My eyes widened. Dot and Mum gasped in horror.

There lay, in neat little packages upon the patio, every single pansy, wallflower and begonia that Mum and Dot had spent over two hours planting. It had taken Katie only a matter of minutes to uproot the lot and place them into tidy piles. She's clever - isn't she?

Signing off for now
Cha Cha

The Christening

Sunday - Dad's day of rest usually. But today Mum and Dad have their early morning cup of tea in bed and mumble grudgingly about having to get up soon, even though Goldie is lying across Dad's feet and they've gone dead, he complains. They are on about some long trip - a Christening - whatever that is. And we are to be left!

Dot, our usual dog-sitter, has gone on a coach trip to the coast with her club and left Katie, my sister, with us. Who's looking after us then?

Mumbles from the bed about the dogs being all right on their own for a few hours, and Eilene and Preston, E&P, from up the road coming to let us out in the garden.

So, we have to be shut in while they go out on an enjoyable jaunt. Well, at least I hear, after giving them a seriously evil look, that we are to be walked before they leave...

With my fluffy, spruce clean white coat I trot along, head held high, indignant, slightly ahead of the other five Poodles. Katie is on her best behaviour as usual, creeping up to be in Dad's best books, walking along off the lead like an angel while everyone else is sniffing about for

interesting stories. They are busy chatting, oblivious to how upset we all are about being deserted on our favourite day at home, when they are both in and we get lots of cuddles all day and a good helping of the Sunday roast with our dinner. I put my nose in the air in disdain. And...

Mum calls out in alarm. Too late! I've already got the whiff of a spot of fun. "Hey girls," I squeal with delight, "RABBITS!"

We've gone. I'm not looking back to witness their faces of utter despair. They don't care about abandoning us after all. We need to be as quick as lightening. I can hear the others yelping behind me as we start to catch up with the rabbits. I feel my blood heating up as the chase progresses. This is what we were designed for - hunting ... retrieving ... Got you! I'll take you back to show Mum. She'll be right pleased, I'm sure, to see how I have retained through the generations the instinct to hunt.

She's screaming about something! Was it the other girls racing up to investigate? No, it's something incoherent about the poor rabbit and my fluffy white coat being splattered all down the front with mud (and my legs, where I misjudged the dyke and landed in the middle of a putrid, muddy bog, brown to the elbows). Mum insists I drop the

rabbit and it scurries off without a care in the world. She says they are probably used to our antics by now but we shouldn't catch them all the same. And she complains that she can't go out and leave my precious show coat splattered with mud and goodness knows what else! There's mention of a bath. A bath! I didn't think Mum had time for that! But in I go. And, frantic, out they go in the most shocking hurry, mumbling "we are going to be late for the Christening."

Us girls get down to a good sleep and, before we know it, E&P from down the road have arrived. Let's knock them flying as they come through the door shall we girls. I'll go first... I'll dig down their pockets - see if there are any sweets.

E&P want us to go out into the garden. I'm not going. I know what it will be - as soon as I've been out there a minute they will take off and leave us again. Better to refuse to go for a while. At least until they both go out with the promise of a game and sweets if I co-operate. Oh well...

I knew it. Out for two minutes. Now they want us back in! Katie has turned awkward. She won't come in. No way. Not for them! Well,

I can tell them now, it's absolutely no use chasing her round the garden. I've never seen P so flushed and out of puff - mind you, I have never seen Preston run that fast before. I didn't know he had it in him. And Katie! Well, that's the widest grin I've seen on her face for a long time. In fact, she hasn't looked so contented since her Mum's jealous boyfriend told her she had to choose between him and Katie. "On your bike!" Dot told him, quite rightly.

Seeing Preston on the verge of a heart attack I decided to go and have a private word in Katie's ear. Mum wouldn't be too pleased if the dog-sitter ended up in casualty. Katie followed me indoors like a lamb once I told her about bits of cheese being sliced in the kitchen and handed out to those coming to get it.

The afternoon passed - frankly it was so hot we were content to sleep the time away and, soon enough, Mum and Dad were back, coming in with arms stretched and gooey talk - they had missed us. We had missed them too, even if we had had a good laugh teasing E&P.

Mum bent down and gave me a good hug. "Oh I have missed you, Cha Cha, I have been telling everybody all about you." I licked her face. She told me she and Dad had discussed my startling antics of the morning on the way down to the Christening and decided that, on reflection, rather than the "horrible creature" (and worse) she called me this morning, I was really rather clever catching a wild rabbit. It meant if I ever got lost I would never starve. Lost! Me! As if I'd ever go that far away from her. I always see her from the corner of my eye. And as for killing the rabbit, no way! I only meant to have a spot of fun chasing it. I think Mum realised that now but she said I wasn't to do it again. In future she would take a ball with us and if I wanted to play chase I must chase that. Fair enough.

Mum collapsed into an armchair while Dad put the kettle on. "Put your feet up love," he told her. But I had my head on them. I like to lay near her like this, with my head on her feet. Feet? Her feet still bore those cosy slippers she'd put on in her mad rush this morning, after her bath - after mine... That was unusual! Normally, when she went out she always put on nice shoes. Oh well, perhaps it didn't matter if people wore bedroom slippers to a Christening!

Signing off for now
Cha Cha

Diana

Sunday 31 July 1997. Today was a specific date in history, a day that will stay in my memory always. The strangest day I have ever known, certainly the saddest day.

Mum got up early to a dark sky. She remarked that she was glad it wasn't raining. It was obvious she was going out on her own. I watched her body language, which suggested detachment and a certain amount of guilt. She refused to look me in the eye so I knew she was wishing she was taking me but couldn't. When she dressed in her red trouser suit I knew she was going to a dog show - and wasn't taking me. I was rather upset about that but at least Dad would take us all for a nice walk. As it turned out, Mum went off to Birmingham with Chris to show 'Bobby Dazzler', my cousin. It seems that I was meant to go but somehow Mum had forgotten to post the entry form.

Dad was at home for the day with me and the other girls and knowing Dad was not one to take us for a walk very early Beryl, Goldie and Tory stayed asleep on the bed in the spot they declared theirs as soon as Mum vacated it. Me, my paternal Mum, Velvet, and my sweet Auntie Penny (so sweet she's on the jacket of one of Mum's books), followed Dad downstairs just after eight. Missing Mum already but having to accept our lot, we watched, only in half expectancy, while Dad filled the kettle from the tap, switched it on, got some bread from the bread bin and popped it into the toaster. He then absently switched on the radio. There was no music, only a strange silence, which seemed to last for ages.

A shiver of emotion seemed to fill the air. Almost immediately the kitchen seemed chill and austere. A man's voice - deep, precise, clear and immensely serious - the most chilling tone of voice I have ever heard, was saying something that was holding Dad spellbound. He was standing as still as a statue, silent as a mouse. It was easy to sense something very terrible and irreversible had happened. As if to confirm my thoughts, Dad suddenly made a rush to the living area and switched on the television, his face was a frozen white, his mouth drooping at the sides, his eyes were instantly filled with moisture.

Staggering backwards as the picture and stilted words of a reporter appeared on the screen, Dad lowered his body down onto the settee, sitting forward with his elbows on his knees and his head resting in his hands. He was trying to say something but words failed him. He was totally incoherent.

Velvet couldn't bear to see Dad so upset; she crawled up beside him and rested her head in his lap. He hardly noticed. I lay with my head on his feet and Penny curled up beside him. As if sensing tragedy Goldie, Tory and Beryl came downstairs on tip-toe, looked questionably at Dad, who had his eyes glued to the television, then quietly sat down as near to him as possible.

The man on the square box wore a solemn expression of disbelief. He kept shaking his head when he spoke as if he didn't actually believe what he was saying and any minute now he would wake up and realise that he had merely been experiencing a nightmare. Dad's frown deepened and he sat back into the sofa as if he needed support. I have never known him so introverted and numb. He was for some reason stunned, like the newscaster, into immobility. I got a little closer to him and Velvet got completely on his lap. Penny moved closer and we all sat there, squashed together like we were trying to get into a picture for a photo-call. Whatever had happened was serious and it had upset our Dad terribly as it was being relayed repeatedly on the television. The staid words of the presenter made everything in the room stand still, as if frozen in time. As if we were all in a photograph and not living souls.

The time passed in static silence but for the television and the droning, depressed voice of the presenter. The only thing I can remember Dad saying was that he wondered if Mum had heard the dreadful news yet. He was worried about how upset she would be. I have never known Dad like this. None of us had. We were almost frightened to move in case he broke.

Dad never moved away from the television. His toast popped up and was forgotten. Little jobs he had told Mum he wanted to do today, like trimming the edges of the lawn, were forgotten. We didn't even get our walk. But somehow none of this mattered. It seemed essential to stay in a sort of animated suspension - a time warp. Something, whatever it was, the man on the radio and then on the television had broadcast, had somehow changed everything. Something dreadful and tragic had touched the world.

Later, Mum came in and found us all in our little group. We were so pleased to see her, perhaps she would cheer Dad up and shake him from his reverie of despair. She cuddled us all in turn with moisture-filled eyes. Dad stood up and came towards her. He locked her in his arms as tears rolled from the corner of her cheeks, down her face until it was drenched. She huddled into his broad chest and they stood still and close like this for some time.

At last Dad prised Mum from the depth of his heart and held her away. "We had better have a stiff drink or some tea with sugar in it." She nodded.

"Everybody has been in deep shock today. Everyone at the show has been crying all day. I have never seen sadness like it. The show went on but it was as if we were all just so stunned we couldn't believe it was true. We tried to be normal but it didn't work. The show was silent and sad. Everybody was sad, sad, sad. Full of sadness, full of disbelief, there were words of love and affection about the person most treasured by understanding people throughout the world. The grief is beyond belief and yet understandable. I doubt another person has ever been so loved and adored, or ever will be again. To have been so misused and then to have life end this way."

Mum insisted we all get some fresh air. We were taken for a long walk out to the sea. We stood and watched the waves flapping against the great defences of the land and wondered at life going on no matter what. We went home feeling as though we must move on, but it was obvious Mum and Dad were struggling inside to sustain their positive attitude. Mum fed us and chivvied Dad into starting dinner. Neither of them had eaten all day. Then we all sat around the television again, with them holding hands. We sat like this until bedtime. It was the strangest and most emotive day ever. "Something, causing deep grief to so many," Mum said. "We will always remember in our hearts and our minds the lovely, caring lady who has been so tragically taken today. A woman who knew, understood, had experienced the pain of love and rejection, saw the pain of others, who knew how to give from her heart."

She was the People's Princess, Princess Diana.

Signing off for now
Cha Cha

Kissy

Bank Holiday Monday - Stella and Beatnick came to tea, (we call him that on account of his long hair). They brought Kissy, my seven year old cousin, who had gone to live with them just a couple of weeks ago, and Ben, their eight year old Golden Retriever.

We all had a fun walk over the Marsh, walking out to the sea to show Stella and Beatnick the seals, and then back for a lovely dinner and a good afternoon nap. I have to say Kissy is a different girl to that crazy, mixed-up Standard Poodle of six weeks before, when Mum and Dad took her in because she had been suddenly rejected after her owner had a baby.

"How anyone could part with Kissy, I'll never know. She is the sweetest thing alive. Such an angel," Stella commented with tears in her eyes. "We love her to bits, don't we dear?"

Beatnick nodded thoughtfully but there was a moment of reserve. "Angel?" he queried. "What about the other day when I had collapsed into a chair and you gave me that big chunk of pork pie?" He looked at Dad for sympathy. "I had it in my hand like this...." he displayed, leaning back with his arm over the side of the armchair. "I only looked away for a second and the pie was gone! I never felt a thing, Kissy swiped it as gently as....as an...."

"Angel," Stella laughed. "Bless her."

"And," he told Dad, as though Dad would understand, "I had only got up for a you-know-what in the middle of the night and when I got back Kissy was in my place in the bed. Under the duvet, would you believe?" Dad nodded sympathetically. "I couldn't move her; she was a dead weight. I had to go and sleep in the spare room!"

"Bless her," Stella murmured lovingly. "Kissy was feeling insecure. She's much better now. She eats well. The first day or two the only thing she was interested in eating, it seemed, was poor Pushea."

Mum drew in a sharp intake of breath. She knew just how precious Stella's cats were to her. Stella read Mum's expression of concern.

"Yes, I was rather upset at the time, to put it mildly. But then I realised Kissy had probably never lived with a cat before, so we set about a gentle and strategic progress of cat/dog socialisation. Firstly we put the cats into a cage whenever they came into the house. Kissy

never left the cage for about three days, then she got bored and took to seeking more active interests, like trying to bite the postman's fingers off when he shoved the mail through the letterbox. We had to put a box on the front gate like you have on yours. The postman doesn't come into the front garden at all now."

"Kissy took to prancing about in the living room - in the middle of the night!" Beatnick said, shaking his head with some disbelief.

Stella laughed. "Bless her. I knew she was up to something no good because Ben had his head under the bedside table trying to hide. I crept silently down the stairs to investigate. Kissy had not one, but two, toilet rolls which she was tossing in the air and throwing from one side of the room to the other."

"I have never known a dog so full of mischief. I must admit when we made that frantic 'phone call to you a few weeks back and you said without reserve that Kissy would settle down soon I didn't believe a word of it. Stella had more faith," Beatnick admitted.

Stella bit her lip. "I have had to change my job. I find Kissy gets up to most mischief when she's been left more than two hours. I go to work earlier now, and come home earlier."

"And I'm home later and come home earlier," Beatnick told us. "The dogs are hardly left on their own at all."

"And I walk them before I go and when I come home. And Ben's

happier now," Stella added quickly. "He is not such a slob now. Kissy won't let him be lazy. She adores him and wakes him up with kisses, then pokes him with her paws to play. Like she does with us in the middle of the night. After we had had her for about a week they would run up and down the stairs practically all day long. I thought she would be tired at night. But she still couldn't sleep. She was like a coiled spring - a caged animal suddenly set free. Bless her," Stella said proudly. "She's much fitter now, and she doesn't bolt under the table or flee upstairs when friends pop round. She acted as if she were never allowed in the house. At first, we had to carry her in from the garden because she wouldn't come over the step. She would stand as still as a statue, refusing to move."

Kissy got up from the armchair where she had been snoozing since we got back from our walk and came to sit next to Stella, leaning her warm body against Stella's legs. Her dark eyes were full of love and contentment. I had never thought to see her eyes with such sweet happiness in them again after the trauma she had suffered. Stella looked at Mum with her face crumpling, her eyes full of moisture. "When she looks at me like that I can never think about telling her she's naughty. In fact, Kissy wouldn't be Kissy if she didn't get into mischief." Stella put her arms around Kissy's neck and kissed the soft skin of her face. Kissy looked across to Beatnick and you could see the smile on her face. She left Stella and moved towards him with her head high and her expression sensitive and submissive. She knew how to get around him.

Beatnick smiled at her. The seduction was complete. "This dog has caused more upheaval in our lives over the past few weeks than I would have thought possible. But," his voice trembled as Kissy touched the rough whiskers of his unshaven cheek with a gentle brush of her beautiful soft face, "I can't imagine life without her now. Bless her."

Signing off for now
Cha Cha

The Launderette

Tuesday - Dad's gone off to work early. Over breakfast (we had my favourite gluten-free meal with a little grated cheese sprinkled on top. Mum had her usual diced banana, apple, sunflower and pumpkin seeds with creamy organic yoghurt) Mum began to mumble to herself. "It's no good," a deep sigh, then.... "I am just going to have to do it!"

I gave her a sideways glance. Whatever she was going to have to do did not involve us dogs. She looked drearily into space as she spoke and not at any of us six.

"I have been putting it off! I should have done it at the beginning of the Summer when the weather was warm... Well. It's no good; I can't put it off any longer. The nights are getting chilly and we are going to need that duvet."

A clue - duvet!

Mum went upstairs after breakfast with a large black bin liner. We all followed. She went into a spare room, opened a cupboard, then proceeded to struggle - with a red face and odd exclamations of frustration - to fold up and stuff into the bin liner the big, thick winter duvet that I remember her taking off the bed back in the Spring. Eventually she sat, exhausted, on the end of the bed, perspiration on her brow, and breathed out a deep breath. "Got you!" she said. "Trying to get that thing in a bag is worse that trying to get a cover on it!" Then she looked at me. "I think I'll take you with me Cha Cha. I don't much fancy a trip to the launderette on my own. You never know who you might meet!"

Mum parked the car outside a shop and we went in. There was a row of washing machines like the one we have in the Utility room at home, plus two more that looked huge in comparison. A row of chairs ran down the middle of the room, washing machines either side. Mum chose one of the larger machines, stuffed the duvet into it with her liquid washer and sat on one of the chairs opposite with a sigh of relief. She looked quite pleased with herself. Rather as I had done after digging up that smelly old bone last week. "I'm glad there's nobody else in here," she told me as she settled back into her chair. "I hate launderettes." I climbed onto the chair next to her and leaned against her shoulder.

We sat like this for ages. Watching the duvet going round and round, first one way, then the other. I was just about to nod off when suddenly the front door flew open. With a crashing bang the door trembled against its hinges. Mum and I stared. A big lady with wide staring eyes stood in the doorway seemingly considering the situation. She glowered at Mum as though she shouldn't be there, and then looked at me with a sort of curious disgust.

She pointed a fat finger towards me. "That blooming thing don't worry me!" Her voice sounded like she had been eating gravel. Mum mumbled something about 'meths' under her breath.

The unusual lady looked even more unusual on account of her clothes. Her attire was reasonable but her dress was a bit too small for her and her cardigan, crying out for an iron, was strained to the limit across her ample bosom, buttons pulled to capacity. On her feet she wore trainers with seemingly purpose-cut peeping toes. She was dragging behind her a shopping trolley. I could see Mum struggling not to stare. I had no such reserve.

The trolley she pulled carelessly behind her came in with a bang and knocked the glass in the front door. It trembled but the strange lady didn't seem to notice. She gave Mum a piercing look and then poked her face into mine. "That err thing a Poodle?" she asked, getting her face close enough for me to lick. I refrained. Mum nodded. The woman threw back her head and roared, as if some huge joke she knew about was forthcoming. "What's it sitting on the.... chair for?" She laughed with zest. "Looks like a blooming person."

I could see Mum had closed her eyes and was pretending to be asleep. The woman sat down on the chair next to me. I wrinkled my nose. I wonder what she bathed in this morning? A black finger-nailed hand stretched my way. I wondered if these dark nails got her extra points like mine did when I was in the show ring. Somehow pale-pink nails look more attractive on people.

The woman stroked my head and then, pointing to the big washing machine in front of Mum, asked "That yours?" She didn't wait for a reply. "I got one of them covers from 'ere last year. Right warm an' all it is."

Mum opened her eyes and nodded. If the woman had known Mum like I did, she would have realised that behind the blank expression was a mind ticking over with awareness and thought.

The big bag lady sat for a moment longer then got up, dragging her trolley in her wake. She went to the first washing machine that had stopped its cycle. Lifting the lid she pulled out the washing, looked intently at each item and put one or two bits into her trolley, casting the other items into the white washing basket on the back shelf. Once she was satisfied with sorting this load she moved on to the next washing machine.

I could now see Mum was staring, wide-eyed, mouth hung. I gave her a nudge. Mustn't stare. But she was mesmerised by the antics of the clamorous, rather ostentatious lady. Our new friend cared not. She carried on, with zest, her odious task.

Our machine suddenly stood still. The woman stared at it with serious contemplation. Mum leaped up, nearly making me jump out of my skin. She seized the door, wrenched it open, grabbed the duvet, called me to follow her and out we went in a rush. Mum not even stopping to put the duvet into her black bin liner.

"What a dreadful experience we've had this morning in the launderette. Some dreadful woman was taking other people's clothes, without a care in the world!" Mum told aunt Dot when we called in on the way home. "That's the last time I go to a launderette." She went on to tell Dot all about the eventful visit. Katie, my sister, was jumping about in her usual ecstatic mood, only more so, not knowing whether to try to lick Mum to death or jump around me with her front down, bottom in air. I could see she was wildly excited about something. She told me, in bunny-hops of promoting activity, "Have I got something to show you!" I couldn't wait to see what stimulus had induced this emission of excess energy. (Not that it takes much to get Katie in a fun mood.)

Rushing into the kitchen, Katie made for a cat box under the kitchen table and then she proceeded to poke about inquisitively with her nose. Her whole body was quivering with excitement. Nose sniffing, I asked what she had got there that was so interesting.

All of a sudden something rushed out from under a blanket and hurriedly scrambled across the kitchen carpet towards the back door. I stood back in awe. Katie went after the thing, touching what looked like a yellow-brownish, mottled, cloudy hard shell. "Good grief - what is it?" Was it some sort of clockwork toy? No, this strange object had a smell to it that wasn't plastic. I watched in wonder as its scaly, leathery legs and head retracted into the shell of its body, like it was magic. It's head and tail disappeared from sight.

Mum and Dot came into the kitchen after us. Dot said, "Here's my tortoise. Isn't it sweet? Katie loves it." Mum looked a bit nonplussed to me. Dot gently chastised Katie. "Leave Tommy alone and take Cha Cha into the garden to play. And don't get up to any mischief." Who, us?

Mum was still on about her ordeal in the launderette when I followed Katie out into the garden. Katie was bursting with excitement even now. "I must show you this other new thing!"

"Oh!" I exclaimed with sheer delight, sniffing at a shimmering shallow spread of water. "Katie, you have got a paddling pond!"

"Yes. Isn't it divine? And there's a little boy, stiff as concrete, with water spurting from a protrusion."

I put my nose under the water and it sprayed everywhere. Katie laughed as it splashed her back, so I did it again. She raced around in glee and came back for more. "Fancy Dot getting you this lovely splash pool, Katie, I wish my Mum would get us one. It's just wonderful on a hot day like today."

Katie jumped sideways as I put my head under the spurting water and we both got soaked. She said "I couldn't believe it when I saw what the men from the garden centre had done. However, my Mum's got some funny ideas. She will keep calling it a fishpond. And every time I go near she tells me to leave it!"

I was sympathetic. "They can be very odd sometimes."

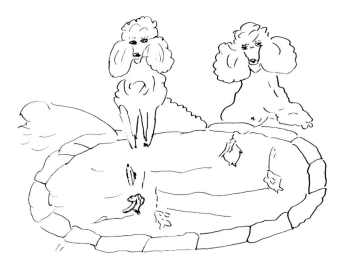

Katie decided with Dot not there to say "leave" it was time to fully explore the pond. We were both thoroughly wet anyway. She, without what one could call lady-like daintiness, put her front feet in the pond and pawed at the shimmering bubbles. Movement immediately caught my eye. "Quick. Look here Katie. I saw something rush beneath the surface of the water."

A jump, splash and noses poking into the water we squealed with delight! Bright orange slippery things darted away from our legs and avoided our tongues. Oh! But it was such fun trying to catch them. We gurgled and sneezed when water went up our noses and over our heads. Try as we might, these strange jet-propelled things were too fast for us to catch, yet they did sometimes leap feet high out of the water.

Suddenly I heard Mum's voice. It was a cry of utter despair! "Oh my goodness! What are you two up to now?"

"Katie! Really!" Dot exclaimed. Katie had the grace to look every-so-slightly guilty, her lips tightened and her face turned away from the pond, as if to say, 'it was nothing to do with me!'

Mum said she was dreadfully sorry about the mess and would put me straight into the back of the car without delay. This she did with little thought and a despairing slam of the door, mumbling about my filthy, muddy feet, muddy, soaking coat, and the poor fish, and was I never going to grow up!

I didn't mind, not really, she'd get over it. And, the duvet she had thrown in here, in her panic when we had left the launderette, was actually quite comfortable.

Signing off for now
Cha Cha

Feng Shui

Thursday. "Sweetheart," Mum said to Dad in a seductive whisper as he buried his face in her sweet-smelling, freshly washed hair. "I want some extra housekeeping money this week."

"For anything in particular?" (I could see by that certain expression of his that she was about to get whatever she wanted.)

"It's like this. Either we have a new duvet or you volunteer to take the present one to the launderette."

"But I thought you said you took it the other day? You said you met some dreadful woman who was pilfering clothes from the machines."

"Yes. But things have deteriorated since then," she said, taking in a sharp intake of breath and glancing at me. Dad's eyes followed hers.

"I had better not ask. But why do I get the feeling this involves Cha Cha?"

"It's a long story. And involves Katie as well." No doubt she would tell him later about our investigative venture into the fish pond, the muddy holes we dug and my consequent spoiling of the freshly laundered duvet with my muddy paws and wet, muddy body!

"If it involves Cha Cha and Katie, say no more!"

"Are you prepared to take a trip to the launderette or scrap the duvet?"

He prised himself from her, opened the kitchen dresser draw, pulled out his cheque-book and said, "How much do you want?" Then he added "I suppose I could stop the sum from Cha Cha's pocket money."

Mum laughed. She gave him one of those looks - which I had better not go into. He signed a cheque and handed it over. Then he sought the sanctity of an armchair while Mum put the kettle on. I climbed onto his lap, laying my paws around his neck and slurped a long kiss across the rough unshaven skin on his face. "You don't have to be all that grateful Cha Cha," he laughed. But I could see that he was tickled pink by the attention. He's such a walkover!

"As a matter of interest," Dad inquired of Mum, "what are you going to do with the old duvet?"

"That's easy. I thought I would cut it into four and make new Feng Shui coloured covers for each section. For the dogs."

"Fen who?"

"Feng Shui, you know, blue, cream and yellow. It's the thing now,

these Colours of the Chinese art of placement. They are supposed to induce harmony with nature, bring you money, luck, happy relationships and good health."

"Harmony!" Dad exclaimed. "Harmony, in a household full of Standard Poodles which, incidentally, happens to include Cha Cha?"

"Oh! She's an angel really, at times," Mum retorted amicably.

"Money! This lot cost me a fortune. Bring luck? Just my luck you choose to visit the launderette on the very day and hour that the local waif does her pick-pocketing!" Dad looked suspiciously cautious. "Why do I get the feeling that rather than save you money, this latest fad of yours is going to cost me money and cause me work?"

"Oh, it won't cost that much. And I only want you to paint the kitchen yellow. There's not much work in that. We don't have that much wall showing."

"And?"

"Of course, we will need new curtains and blinds."

"Naturally. In blue, cream or yellow?"

"Orange actually."

Dad rubbed his chin with the tips of his fingers. He was obviously deep in thought. "And, because the dining area is adjacent to the kitchen, the walls will be the wrong colour; and there's the possibility that the carpet will not prove harmonious?"

Mum had the good grace to smile guiltily. "Well, yes."

Dad glanced at her and then at me, still sitting on his lap. With a wry grin he said, "and I suppose the Chinese believe that the dog is a creature that keeps watch and is skillful in warding away anyone who is not what they may appear to be."

Mum gasped. "How did you know that?"

Dad tilted his head to one side as he smiled. "Well, it just so happens that when I went into the bathroom for a bath and shave, Cha

Cha came trotting in carrying something in her mouth - the magazine you have been reading today, so it seems. I rescued it from her and the article where it was folded over caught my eye. I read it. That's why I didn't get to complete my ablutions before you called me for dinner."

Mum exclaimed and came to scuff him softly with her hand. "Then you knew all about Feng Shui all the time?"

"Well, I didn't know then that the reason Cha Cha was carrying the magazine about in her mouth was because she wanted me to read it, as you had discussed with her your plans for the duvet."

Mum told him, as she pushed me aside to share his lap, "The dogs need some new duvets and if I cut the old one into four I will be able to get the pieces into our washing machine."

Dad stroked me. "Well, then I really have reason to thank Cha Cha. I have only got to buy one large duvet and not four."

I rested my chin on his shoulder and sighed contentedly. He smiled at me and Mum followed his eyes and smiled at me too. This Feng Shui thing obviously works, for we were at harmony once again.

Signing off for now
Cha Cha

Bathing with Bobby

All puppies are lovely, soft, sweet-smelling, cuddly and totally irresistible. Bobby, at eight weeks old, was a bundle of black fluff with beautiful eyes that were as black as coal - eyes that followed you everywhere. He was a puppy full of uncomplicated love and utter devotion. Mum said she had no intention of keeping a male from

Goldie's litter of five puppies, not with all us females around, but I could see it was becoming increasingly difficult for her to even contemplate parting with this black bundle of joy. He idolised her and she him. He was getting cuddled continuously and spoiled rotten!

Two different couples wanting a show dog came to see this lovely stunner that Mum called 'Bobby'. And no wonder they wanted him, he had the presence of royalty about him from the moment he could stand up. The bearing and carriage one recognises and describes in dogs as 'star quality'. Mum, on the brink of tears, looking sheepishly at Dad, turned both couples down. But she was in a dilemma - she told Dad how difficult it would be to keep an entire male with us five girls. "He would have to be shut away when they are in season etc." Dad was no help. He said they could manage somehow if she loved Bobby that much.

Then Mum's sister, Aunt Sylvia, came to call. She's got Rio (a white boy from Goldie's other litter two years ago) and Ben (a black boy from Beryl ten years before). She wasn't even contemplating another puppy yet. But she took one look at Bobby and I could see her heart melt. The same gooey look came to her face as it did to Mum's when she picked Bobby up to cradle him in her arms. He collapsed back and laid contentedly murmuring sweet nothings at her while dreamily looking deeply into her eyes. She kissed his face and he sighed. Aunt Sylvia said "I'm taking him home!"

I could see Mum was overjoyed and she willingly gave Bobby to her much loved sister. He went to live not far away at all with Sylvia, her husband Bill, their teenage offspring Debbie and Natasha, and Rio and Ben.

Bobby grew but he never changed. He's every bit as gorgeous as he ever was. As Bill has said to Mum on many occasions, "He is perfect but for one or two things. The trouble is he does have this passion for water! We were hoping that he would grow out of it, and we did think....but we should have realised.... if anything he has got worse, and too clever!"

Sylvia sipped on the tea Mum handed her, put her cup down on the patio table and shook her head. "I was baking cakes and Bill was playing landing aeroplanes on the computer when suddenly loud shrieking screams came wailing up the hall from the bathroom. We both dropped everything  and rushed along the hall of the bungalow, arriving at the source together. The screams, still piercing our ear drums, were inflected with intonations of blasphemy, impious words, half obscured by little gulps of hysterical laughter."

"Bobby," Bill explained, "after digging for Australia in one of Sylvia's prized flower beds, had secured a good octopus rooted plant whose tentacles were grasping onto the mud which cherished them. He had seized the plant and run indoors with it to show everyone how clever he was when he had been distracted mid-stream by the sound of running water coming from the bathroom. Diverted, muddy plant still in mouth, he went to investigate."

Debbie was shouting, crying, and laughing. "He.... that.... dog pushed open the door, hesitated for about one second, his eyes growing into bright, wide marbles of delight, then took one single leap from the doorway, landing four square in the bath with me, and started to dig for the soap!"

"My goodness!" Sylvia exclaimed to Mum. "You should have seen the mess. The plant in the bottom of the bath oozing brown mud sediment, splattered bath water all over the floor, up the tiles and even splashed on the ceiling! A sopping wet Bobby tremendously pleased with himself, and Debbie, still sitting in the bath, hysterical, filthy with splattered mud. Bobby was doing his best to wash her tear-drenched face with his long wet tongue. Bill and I didn't know whether to laugh or cry."

Mum bit on her lower lip guiltily. I think she had had a suspicion all along that Bobby had another side to that demure, sweet innocence he projected. "He is lovely in some ways," she offered quickly in a desperate attempt to save Bobby's grace, "he loves children."

"Yes," Bill said "and don't we know it! Especially small children." It was his turn to shake his head in despair. "Bobby is not satisfied with our teenagers; he wants to play with the three young boys next door. Trouble is, they will entice him, talking to him through the fence and screeching with laughter when he jumps the fence to join them playing football."

Sylvia told us, "Bill spent all Saturday and Sunday raising the height of the fence. He even put a rail along about eight inches from the fence to deter Bobby jumping at it, like Roy suggested. When he was finished Bill and I stood back, well satisfied. 'There, that will keep the little blighter in,' we said. We went back indoors and about five minutes later there were shrieks of laughter coming from next door. We sort of knew the source immediately and went to see - what next! We couldn't believe our eyes. Bobby, not being physically capable of jumping six foot from a standstill with a bar in the way, had climbed up a tree and come out through the thick green branches of the conifer on the other side. We caught a view of his head coming through just before he jumped and landed amongst his young playmates next door."

"I won't tell you what I threatened him with," Bill said.

"He gets threatened with all kinds of unprintable words," Sylvia commented, "but then we sit down in the evening to watch television and he sits contentedly on the sofa pushing his warm body against us. He glances up at us with those dark, loving eyes and looks as though butter wouldn't melt in his mouth. The utter devotion of an innocent puppy!"

Oh well, all's well that ends well.

Signing off for now
Cha Cha

Sad

There's a stranger in the camp, a white bitch about the same age as me (just over twelve months) and about the same height. At first sight I thought she was fat but, on closer inspection, I realised her coat gave her that impression. It was a mass. Not like my coiffure at all. More like the dense woollen coat of the sheep in the field up the road. Mum put her hand on the stranger's back and winced. There were tears in her eyes.

"The woman said, when I went to fetch her, that she didn't want to feed the bitch too much in case it made her want to go to the toilet. There was no garden at all," she told Dad.

Dad tried to stroke the stranger but her black eyes stared like marbles and her nostrils flared like a petrified horse. She shivered and shrank away from him like he was some sort of ogre and fled to sanctuary beneath the kitchen table.

I went to tell the stranger he was all right, our Dad, when I saw she was piddling on the carpet.

"Sheer fright," Mum said as she got a mop and bucket.

"It's a sad state of affairs," Dad murmured with a sigh as he shook his head in despair. "To see any dog reduced to such a cringing condition as that is heart wrenching. What has happened to her that she has lost all her natural spirit, pomp and dignity? It's very sad indeed."

That's how the stranger's name became 'Sad'.

Mum took Sad into the grooming room and spent three hours clipping off her tangled mess of matted coat and bathing her. Sad looked like a sheared lamb. But, as Mum said, it would have been extremely painful and cruel to comb out that felted mass. At least Sad was left with a reasonably creditable topknot, and as Mum said, the hair would grow. And Sad certainly smelt nicer. Mum said what she was more worried about was the dejection and sorrow in Sad's eyes than her short hair-do.

Sad came out of the grooming room with a different look and smell about her and, perhaps, feeling a little less depressed. Dad didn't try to touch her; he just he told her, in that deep, gravely, seductive voice of his, just how pretty she looked. I could see he fractionally impressed Sad even if she didn't want to show it. And when he opened a cupboard and got out a crackling bag which prompted all of us to immediately rush to his side and sit in anticipation of the treat about to come, Sad almost joined us.

Throughout the day Dad kept telling Sad she looked good with her new hair-do and that she had a pretty face, using his most captivating and beguiling voice (the one he usually reserves for whispering certain words in Mum's ear that puts a smile on her face and a certain look in her eyes). Sad, I could see, was beginning to respond to him. As the day wore on she began to hold her head higher and she seemed to have a distinct resemblance of a bounce in her step.

Sad was impressed with Mum and Dad and, after a little encouragement from me and the rest of the family, she joined us in a meal. She was certainly less suspicious of us other Standard Poodles than she was of humans. The meal, served to us all in separate stainless steel dishes was delicious - meat topped with chicken and vegetables in tantalising gravy. We all had a raw bone for afters. Sad didn't know what to do with hers - she carried it about in her mouth for about an hour. Her attitude became more proud as Mum and Dad laughed at her. The other girls and I played the game of teasing her for her wares. Sad would only have to open her mouth and let that bone drop and it would disappear into the nearest waiting mouth.

Being instinctively aware that she was in a prime position, Sad held her head higher and a faint sparkle appeared in her eyes. She liked this sense of power. Eventually, however, she lay under the kitchen table and tried chewing at her possession. At last it disappeared. Only just in time - a knock at the front door and....

Eilene and Preston, E&P, our neighbours and friends from up the road popped in for coffee. They gawked at the Whippet-like frame of Sad after we girls had molested them. Their voices were soft and sympathetic and they shook their heads about her predicament of being thrown out and homeless. They said that if they hadn't already got three naughty-but-nice Elkhounds they would give Sad a home. Sad eventually responded to their kindness, as she had with Dad, sniffing hesitantly at their out-stretched hands. At last she allowed them to stroke her back. And then, with a gesture of gratitude, she shoved her nose under Dad's elbow in a tremendous effort to be friends. He responded softly, like he does when any one of us treat him this way. Being well-trained, he stroked Sad's head and caressed her ears. Mum bit her trembling lip, though she looked pleased and encouraged.

Sad began to settle down quite comfortably after a few days. She ate four small meals a day, learned about going for walks and how to stay close to Mum when on a lead. She learned about jumping onto the table in the grooming room but not on the kitchen table. And she learned that human hands in this household were kind.

Then, one night, as Mum and Dad sat up in bed doing the crossword in The Telegraph, Mum said if Sad didn't go soon she was going to be here forever, it would be a wrench to part with her. They couldn't keep all the Rescue dogs that came our way.

The next morning Mum made a bit of an emotional telephone call. That afternoon a middle-aged couple called Pat and Steve came to call. Pat was talkative with a nice round face framed with mousy-brown hair and Steve was tall, athletic looking with dark, silver streaked hair. He reminded me of my Dad with his friendly tone of voice. Pat and Steve sat around the kitchen table with Mum and Dad. They chatted endlessly about Sad and about problems, feeding, walks, settling in, the odd pee... From time to time Sad looked at with them with growing interest and, eventually, she responded to the gentle persuasion in their kind voices and allowed them to stroke her. Amazingly she sniffed Steve and then lifted her paw to him. Pat got out her handkerchief and blew her nose when Sad stood with her front feet on Steve's shoulders and allowed him to caress her tummy.

Sad closed her eyes in dreamlike fashion.

Two hours after Pat and Steve arrived Sad was put onto a lead and she followed them outside. With a little encouragement she jumped onto the back seat of their car.

As the car pulled away over the gravel drive Sad rested her head on the back seat, staring at us all out of the back window. Mum waved at her with tears streaming from her eyes. Dad put his arm around her and murmured something incoherently about if Sad failed to settle she could come back and stay. He pulled Mum into his arms and they walked slowly in doors. We all followed respectfully. We hate it when they are sad.

Mum was like a cat on a hot tin roof for the next two days. She kept saying "I hope Sad is all right." Then, eventually, on the third day, the 'phone call came.

When Dad came home from work and us girls had finished

pestering him Mum was all over him with excitement, much more her usual cheery self. "Pat and Steve called. Guess what? 'Sad' is now called 'Bonnie'. They say she is such a bonny young lady. I can't believe it; they say she is so full of life and full of love. She has

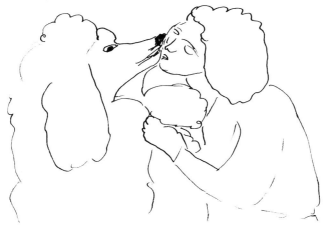

practically demolished the fish pond, chosen to sleep between them in bed, nearly licked the cat to death and runs circles around Patch, their little Terrier.'

Dad and Mum had their tea and then we all went for a lovely walk over the nature reserve. It was great fun and Mum was happier than she'd been for days. I know how worried she was about Sad, 'Bonnie', what a happy name and a happy ending.

We returned home exhausted but smiling. The telephone was ringing. Mum rushed to answer it and her head shook from side to side. "Yes," she said with a sigh. "This is Standard Poodle Rescue. How can we help?"

Signing off for now
Cha Cha

Day-dreaming

Saturday - Dad is in the habit of getting up very early from Monday to Friday so we are all used to getting on the bed for a cuddle with Mum before she vacates the warm spot to get on her computer for an hour or two. Saturday and Sunday they lay in together - unless we are off to a dog show. (Mum says my coat is getting gorgeous now, all her care is paying off.) This morning I can't sleep. I wish they would wake up and get up.

The trouble is I have been dreaming about chasing the other girls over the hills and downs, through the water ponds and darting in and out of trees. Yesterday, Velvet chased a hare and, would you believe, she actually caught it. She grabbed it by the back of it's neck and held her head high to show it off, its wriggling legs dangling. Luckily for it, apart from angelic Penny, the rest of us were not yet detached from our leads so we couldn't get to make it's acquaintance. Goldie and I stood on tiptoe to view the spectacle of little Velvet (as Mum calls her because she is the most petite Standard Poodle imaginable) holding on to the objecting hare with gritted teeth as it fought with incredible activity to gain its freedom.

Mum raised her voice with stern authority. "Velvet...leave. Put that down at once!"

Well, you should have seen the stunned expression on Mum's face when Velvet, glancing directly at her, opened her mouth to drop her prize. The cat-sized hare took off with haste to become a speck in the distance within seconds. Now we are not allowed to chase animals. Shame, but there you go.

When Eilene and Preston (you all know them by now - live up the road - friends - have three naughty-but-nice Elkhounds) came in later for morning coffee, Mum repeated twice, as if still overcome with amazement. "I told Velvet to drop the hare - and she did!" Her eyes wide, her head tilted, "I told her to drop it and like an angel she did! She obeyed without question!"

E&P looked suitably impressed and both commented that perhaps at long last Velvet was 'growing up'. I could see by the twist of Mum's lips that she had reservations. She was not so sure. Anyway, for whatever reason Velvet had for such a sudden willingness to oblige, she wasn't telling any of us. Not even me. I suppose I was dithering upon the subject all night long. I couldn't sleep. And, apart from that, I do like to get up early.

Through a crack in the curtain I could see the first light of day breaking through the dark sky. Soon, the bright sun would appear in friendly fashion and the day would prove cheerful and enticing. September is a nice month. It is still bright and warm but not so hot as to get us dogs into a panting frenzy after a good run over the riverbank or marsh. Being a really nice day may prove even more advantageous. A longer walk out to the sea could be on the cards with intriguing and spectacular birds to watch feeding and diving into the sea, squawking their head off with excitement. These, I might add, are strictly not for chasing. In fact when we walk beside the nature reserve we are kept on leads, but we don't mind. It's a lovely walk and we meet people with their dogs, get lots of pats and observe interesting aspects of natural life. And we are allowed to climb the trees....

I am thinking about these interesting aspects and it make me fidgety. I stand up and softly press my nose against Mum's cheek. I think her mouth twitched but she has got her eyes pressed tight closed, as if she has practised. I know what it is, of course. As soon as she opens her eyes we will all know she is awake and will expect some action.

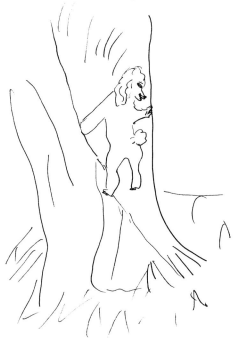

I put my nose under the duvet and start licking her feet. Nuzzling her cheek doesn't get any real response. I gently give a lick on her eyelashes and then stare in her face with a rather sweet, innocent look of an angel. She knows I am there, of course, starring at her like this but she still manages to keep her eyes tightly closed. It's not working. Once she blinks, the night is over.

I sigh deeply. I will have to try plan B. I turn around, playing at getting comfortable, accidentally on purpose, knocking the bed. The mattress wobbles like a jelly. Mum and Dad are always moaning about it and threatening to buy a new bed. Dad sighs and turns over. At least he is semi-awake now. I watch Mum intently but there's nothing doing there, her eyes still as shut tight as the front door.

I can see the sun breaking through now. It penetrates the tiny gap in the curtains like a laser beam, whereupon dance tiny fragments of dust. I try sneezing. No good. How about a good sigh?

Oh no! With a sudden movement Dad wraps Mum in his arms. Blast, now what's he up to?

There's only one thing for it. The final way I know will bring about abrupt attention. I'll get a bit of a distance from the bed and then have a good scratch! I bet that'll do it.

Signing off for now
Cha Cha

Gigi

December - Rain has stopped for the first time in about a week. It seems like years since we all had a good run and, when Mum's not looking, chased rabbits. It's amazing; Goldie has kept clean for more than two days! Things will get back to normal this morning with a bit of luck - now that the weather has changed. Blue sky, bright yellow sun - we will be off for a walk soon. Mum's looking out of the bedroom window with bright, wide eyes and a smile on her face. Goldie is standing beside her, nose pressed against the window pane. I know what she's thinking! "Just let me get out there and run through the puddles and the lagoon. I might even catch a duck."

Luckily, for the ducks that is, Goldie will insist on carrying them  in her soft mouth back across the lagoon, through the wooded copse to the point of the Marsh where Mum and us others have got to on our walk. Mum shakes her head in despair, asks Goldie why she can't forget about her inheritance for once and leave the ducks alone. Mum takes the bird out of Goldie's mouth and sets it free, warning us not to chase it as it takes flight into the sky and back out to its spot on the lagoon, it being non-the worse for Goldie's antics. Now, if it had been a tasty rabbit!...

I think Mum has got used to us hunting for wild rabbits now. She doesn't scream with quite as much desperation and ferocity when we catch one, she's knows we won't harm them. Mind you, she near on had a fit last week when we had Gigi staying with us. Gigi belongs to

Mum's friend Shirley and is a little fluffy apricot pom-pom-adorned Miniature Poodle. Before coming to us she had never been away from home. Dad said she was a six-year-old, couch potato but he made us promise not to tease her about it. The first day of her visit Goldie and I taught Gigi how to race up and down the stairs with a fluffy teddy-bear in her mouth. Then we showed her the trick of jumping over the gate into the paddock, which she mastered with remarkable speed, then how to leap into a muddy puddle and create a good splash.

I must say the other girls and I were pretty impressed with the way this couch potato responded to a dare! To tell you the truth we were surprised at her bravado, as we didn't believe she had it in her. I mean, every time we have seen her - when visiting her Mum - Gigi sat on Auntie's knee being pampered and nursed like a baby, or she clung to Shirley's bosom as though her life depended on her being protected from any form of exercise, fun or manoeuvrability.

Day two of her stay with us, enforced because Aunt Shirley had to go into hospital for an operation, things improved further. Gigi learned to climb our A frame all by herself (with a little help from copying me and with Velvet hot on her tail in a game of tag). Gigi came over the top of the A frame with such speed and with such a smile on her face that we stood back in wonder. I raced in to get Mum, who, after my two woofs, followed me as requested. She was just in time to witness Velvet chasing Goldie (fluffy teddy-bear in mouth) chasing Gigi around the garden, up and over a patio table then up the A frame like a dose of salts! Mum closed her eyes, crossed her fingers with hands clung to her chest, sucked in a sharp intake of air, held her breath - then let out a yell.

But she need not have despaired. Gigi had mastered the art of jumping and landing right on four feet with the swiftness, lightness and daring ability of a master acrobat.

"You should have seen her!" Mum told Dad when he got home from work that evening. "She was brilliant."

He said, lowering himself into a chair before Tory got in first, "Really, are we talking Gigi here - the one of the closeted bosom? Gigi, the one of the silk-sheeted bedroom and satin cushioned lounge, high-rise apartment, who has probably never seen a blade of grass in her life other than the bowling green, or a postage-stamp sized lawn at an afternoon's drinks party, and never run or jumped over a thing in her life? What if she had broken a leg?"

"Well she didn't."

"No thanks to our lot."

"I think I might try taking her for a walk with the girls tomorrow."

Dad looked worried. "I wish you wouldn't. I sense disaster."

Gigi wouldn't walk on a lead. Mum carried her, juggling us on leads with her other hand. I could have told her that now that Gigi had found her feet - so to speak - Mum was asking for trouble.

After about a quarter of a mile Mum became less concerned. She let Gigi down gently, unclipped the lead and told her "Either you walk or you stay there. You may well be only half the size of my girls but you sure get heavy."

Gigi sat and stayed. We walked on, looking forward to being let off for a good run after another quarter of a mile walk along the bank to where we reach the bridle paths.

Gigi sat.

With a sigh Mum said she supposed she ought to go back and fetch her. But she had another sudden inspired thought and slipped my lead off. "Cha Cha - go fetch Gigi."

Bounding with sheer exuberance I reached Gigi in a matter of seconds. I told her, in no uncertain terms, either she races me back to Mum or I grab her round the back of her neck like I do a rabbit and carry her. In fact, I did this for about two paces and suddenly Gigi laughed and wriggled free. She had come to life so I dropped her and of a sudden she was racing ahead of me like a bat out of hell.

Mum praised me for being so clever and I stopped to give her a kiss. Gigi raced on. Yelp. Yelp. Yelp. Yelp...."This freedom is sensational," she shouted in the sail of the wind. Then she caught the whiff of a rabbit! I ran to investigate. But Gigi got there before me. I have to hand it to her, she is as quick as lightening. She tried her best to pick the rabbit up by the scruff of it's neck and at the third attempt she managed it. Probably because I had arrived on the scene and she didn't want me nicking her prize. Gigi struggled with the rabbit until Mum arrived in panting commotion. Mum gasped. "Gigi! Drop that rabbit!"

"Oh my! You should have seen Shirley's face when I told her," Mum said to Dad later that night.

"You went to see Shirley in hospital and told her about Gigi's antics!" Dad was astounded.

Mum nodded. "I know it was rotten of me. And I wasn't going to. But Shirley kept on and on about her having a nervous breakdown with just thinking about her operation. I thought it might be a good idea to give her something else to think about while she was waiting to go down."

"And did it?"

"Well, let's put it this way, I doubt that she needed much anaesthetic!"

Signing off for now
Cha Cha

Dog Talk

I was sitting at the front gate watching the world go by when along came a decidedly panting Tor, the magnificent Elkhound from up the road. Tagging along in  his wake was his equally breathless and puffing owner, Preston. Tor sat down as soon as he saw me and refused to budge. "Do us a favour," he asked me with a pathetic droop in his lip. "Woof your Mum out here, will you?" He cocked his eye upwards towards P. "I need to keep him occupied for a few minutes while I take a breather. I mean, eight years old and never walked more than half a mile in my life, and now he's taken it into his head to run a daily marathon!"

Mum smiled as she came down the drive to see what all the noise was about. "Morning, Preston. I see you have decided to take the doctor's advice and are getting more exercise."

Preston puffed. "And mighty well I was doing, so I thought. The old blood pressure was coming down nicely. I had it almost under control - until I went to a dog show yesterday."

Mum smiled. "Lousy judge?" she guessed.

"I asked the drat man. I said 'Why didn't you give my Beauty

Best of Breed?' He had the nerve to say Beauty had light eyes! Well, 'Dogs don't walk on their....eyes, darling,' I told him."

Mum twisted her lips. "Did you say that?"

"Too right I did. I told the idiot that I had judged the breed last week and ninety per cent of the dogs had light eyes, at least they were no darker than Beauty's. And everyone else said the judge must have something against me because Beauty was the best dog there."

Tor sighed. "He's been doing nothing but moan since he came home from that drat show. You'd think shows were the be all and end all. I don't know why he bothers, all it does is raise his blood pressure."

I told Tor that Mum plays the piano (with our help) to calm her nerves.

Preston rubbed his chin. "I wish I could give it up. But I'm lost if

I don't get to the shows at least once a week," he told Mum. "Every time I retire a dog I decide that's it. And then another pup comes along and people start raving about it and I just know this is the one above all others. I have to get out there and prove it."

Mum stood and listened. Tor looked bored and wasn't ready to proceed with his journey.

"I used to love going to shows, didn't you Tor?" I asked.

He shook his head. "My last experience was enough to put one off for life. I was up against that big-head FF. Forever Fruity. He was boasting that his owner gets more judging appointments than my Dad. 'And we all know why, don't we sweetie?' I said to FF. 'He entertains half the....show committees.' And do you know what? He had the nerve to say I was jealous."

"You! I don't believe it."

"Well there you are. I would have left it at that but FF would go on, boasting that he was going to win and he only needed one more point to get his Junior Warrant Certificate and how he knew he would win that day because his owner had that look on his face. So I dared him to play up a bit, to make things a bit more interesting."

'But I get kisses and bits of sausage if I'm good,' he yelled out.

'Goody two shoes,' I sniggered, "why don't you let somebody else win for a change?'

"And do you know what he said. 'You'll never win anything much while your Dad insists on wearing those unbecoming shell suits and smells of garlic!' I like garlic but anyway I couldn't see what that has to do with it. 'It's supposed to be a dog show, not a fashion show,' I retorted. 'They're supposed to judge the dogs, not the handler.'

'Oh! And since when?'

'At least I don't have to live in a cage,' I retorted. That got him; he went quiet for a bit. But then he snorted, 'The weight you carry about it is obvious you don't get walked far.'

'I do, so there. I get to go for nice walks every day and chase rabbits and things.' Tor was telling fibs but I never said anything. I could see he was in a high passion.

'No wonder your hair's a mess,' FF said with a threatening curl in his lip. 'You often look like you've been dragged through a hedge backwards.'

Tor took a deep breath. "Well that was it; I'd had enough. I took a swipe at the arrogant....so and so. And in doing so knocked poor Dad clean off his feet. He was mystified. He apologised to FF's owner and took me out of the ring. I have been a misunderstood dog ever since."

Poor Tor.

"The worst of it was that Dad came home and put his shell suit in the bin because it got torn in the furore that took place between FF and me. And the following week he bought one of those infuriating tweed jackets like FF's Dad wears."

"By the sound of him now it doesn't seem to have done him a great deal of good." He was positively going at it hammer and tongs to poor Mum .

When we finally walked back to the house together, Mum looked down at me and sighed. "Thanks for that Cha Cha. Next time your friends stop for a chat keep quiet about it, will you?"

I shoved my nose in her hand and she petted me. "You really are a lovely dog," she said. "How would you like to come to another show Cha Cha? I've got itchy feet talking to Preston."

I bounced ahead of her and went to tell the others. "Hope she doesn't wear a shell suit," they said. Well, they had obviously been talking to Tor before me and forgot to mention the fact.

Signing off for now
Cha Cha

A Social Visit

Katie, my sister, said she couldn't understand why her Mum, Dot, was so upset with her for digging up all the plants in the garden again. "At least I caught that drat mole!" Katie said in defiance. The fact that half a ton of soil found its way into the fish pond was something she hadn't contemplated when the light earth scurried beneath her paws and up between her legs.

Katie was with us for the weekend because Aunt Dot had gone to visit her son in Reading. They were going sight seeing.

"In Reading!" my Mum exclaimed to our friend Ann Marie (further up the road than P&E and the owner of seven - words fail me but vocal supreme, nuclear fission, electric charge, comes to mind - Finnish Spitz).

Mum wanted to walk Katie and me on the road on account of our feet, "to get your nails down," so off we three went on the mile hike to the Spitz Den. Tamo, the one of a Crufts win, no less, was overjoyed to see us and more than ready for a friendly chat. He was in the garden on his own, while the girls were all indoors on account of their condition, and he was dying for someone to play with. And we like him. Not only is he like a soft, lovable red teddy bear, he's good for a gossip - never could keep a secret.

"What's up with your coat," he asked Katie when we arrived at the front door and were taken through to play in the desecrated minefield.

"My coat! Who said that my coat was anything other than perfect?" Katie snapped.

I said "Really Katie, you only had a bath yesterday and now you're filthy. No wonder Dot is exasperated."

"Ex.... in a high passion! Over a bit of mud? The fact is I have always fancied being brown like Tamo, instead of blue."

Tamo bristled slightly. "I am red, not brown. And my Mum says it is on account of my red blood that I am so mischievous."

Katie looked alert and listened intently as she was in a rebellious mood. I smiled. "What have you been up to Tamo?"

Tamo shook his head. "I promised Mum I wouldn't tell. You see, she had to get the window cleaner to help her and she is right embarrassed about it."

I reassured him. "I know from listening-in that window cleaners see all sorts of things and are keen to tell. Tamo, half the street will have heard about it by now! So you may as well let on." That was enough encouragement for Tamo. He nodded and a smile broadened his wedge-shaped, handsome face.

"For goodness sake, what does she think I am anyway? I wonder sometimes if she realises I'm a Finnish Spitz. If she wanted a Border Collie why didn't she get one? I mean, she only tried to get me to climb up that terrifying new A frame she has decided she wants us all to master, perched in the back garden."

Katie pulled a face, put her nose in the air. She yawned. "They are so easy to climb, Tamo. Any dog can get up and over the silly things. Easy peasy."

"Maybe to you, but I don't like heights. My Mum can't seem to get it into her head. We spent the entire yesterday morning out in the garden going over and over what I was supposed to do. First she patted the bottom of the frame and the whole thing wobbled; yet she expected me to risk life and limb climbing it. Then she put a piece of liver halfway up and told me to fetch it. What was the point? I knew I'd get a bit for tea anyway, especially if I barked enough."

"Yawn, yawn," Katie said.

I said "Don't take any notice of her, she's in a mood because her Mum's gone off for the weekend when she wanted to go to the beach."

Tamo nodded. I prompted him. "What happened next, did you climb the frame?"

"No way, but Mum did! She got on her hands and knees and woofed, calling me to follow her. Is she mad? There she was standing nonchalantly on the top rung shouting my name and... The next thing, the frame wobbled. Mum panicked and fell. The air was blue, I can tell you. I've never heard the likes of it. She had the A frame between her legs and was screeching with horror about not being able to move for fear of doing herself some severe, permanent damage. I mean, and to think she wanted me to climb it! Where do they get these strange ideas? And after seeing her in that predicament....well...."

"What did you do?"

"I walked away in disgust, cocked my leg up the nearest tree and found an old bone to chew on."

Katie and I smiled. We couldn't help it. "Enter the window cleaner?" Katie said with a twinkle in her eye.

Oh dear, I wonder what Dot's in for next?

Signing off for now
Cha Cha

Christmas Eve

Last year, of course, I was too young to remember much about Christmas. So it was with much excitement I followed Mum upstairs one day to discover she was intent on digging deep into the recess of a cupboard to toss out numerous bags and boxes of all shapes and sizes. Rather like a dog digging a treasured spot to rediscover a prized bone, I thought.

These items she carried downstairs to place on the sitting room floor. Looking around with a deep breath Mum mumbled something about always leaving things to the last minute. Eilene and Preston, our neighbours and friends, were arriving any minute and they were all going out to dinner. Dad was upstairs now putting on his best bib and tucker.

In a hurried manner Mum cleared a small table in the corner of the room, beside the great fireplace. She went to the sideboard, rummaged through a pile of tablecloths and pulled out a bright red one, decorated with lots of small green trees. Then she took hold of a tall narrow box, undid the end and out slipped a long, narrow green object. To my astonishment the thing, manipulated by Mum's slim fingers, blossomed into a green tree! It was like some sort of miracle. I was impressed.

At this point the other girls came in with Dad, seemingly much pleased, with wagging tails and smiling faces, tongues panting. Dad had a dressing gown over his suit and was carrying a basket full of logs. He set this on the hearth. "Doesn't seem five minutes since we put that tree away!"

Mum nodded and said she was a bit worried it might have had it's day. But Dad didn't seem perturbed. "I'm sure it will be all right when it's dressed." Before he left to put the kettle on Mum said something about liking his faith.

Me, Goldie and Velvet sat around the floor watching Mum. Beryl and Tory climbed onto chairs, all eyes on Mum. A box was opened

and out came several brightly coloured, glittering balls on delicate bits of gold cord. Mum lifted each one in turn and hung them on different branches of the tree. They looked nicely interesting, bouncing so daintily. Another box was dived into and startling slivers of delicate glittering silver glinted before my eyes. I put my nose on them but they made me sneeze. Mum said I was to leave, which I quite agreed to do. She then hung these strange silver fragments on branches on the green tree. I thought her behaviour a bit strange although the room did somehow look brighter with this glittering green tree in the corner.

Tory snored. Beryl sighed contentedly. Velvet and Goldie were sitting upright with their backs against the seat of the settee. It was obvious from their expressions they had seen this odd behaviour of Mum's before. I looked on.

Another box, a long green lead with several different coloured little bells were carefully untangled and wrapped around the tree. Mum fiddled with the plug and socket and Hey Presto! Wow. The whole tree lit up into a cascade of blinking, tiny droplets of multi-

coloured lights. Mum looked much pleased and stood back to survey the work. Dad came in with two steaming mugs of coffee. "Lovely," he murmured. He sounded a bit emotional, put the coffee down, put his arms round Mum - oh, surely they are not....

A tap on the front door and E&P came in, parcels in hand. Mum took the parcels and laid them at the foot of the tree while Dad poured E&P a sherry. Eilene and Preston sat on the settee and were piled upon by Tory, Beryl and Goldie. Velvet was too busy looking at the parcels and sniffing to bother with the guests. I said a quick hello then my nose was attracted to a scent wrapped in brightly coloured paper.

Before they left for their dinner party Mum looked very suspiciously at Velvet and me. "I think we had better shut the dogs out of the sitting room tonight. I don't like the curious look on Velvet and Cha Cha's faces," she said to Dad.

"Oh, they'll be all right. I think you're over-reacting."

Velvet and I looked at each other and smiled. We were both still quite young, remember....

Signing off for now
Cha Cha

Introducing Treasle

There are some things that are just too painful to write about. The thing was, there were only six months between Beryl and Tory, and I suppose they had been slowing down quite a bit in the last year but they were always so happy, with wagging tails, that we may not have realised they were the age they were.

Anyway, we were just coming to terms with the sadness of losing our dear friend Beryl when Tory was called to Heaven. It was awful.

Time passed. The house seemed very quiet with just me, Velvet, Goldie and Penny, so Remi came. She's my half-sister and as sweet as you like. She is sparkling white, like me, and that meant Velvet was the only blue amongst us now.

Spring arrived, bringing beautiful bright yellow flower heads and tiny white snowdrops. Dad said the garden looked stunning for a change because pups hadn't demolished it, nor had young, naughty Standard Poodles. Velvet had joined the ranks of the adult-minded and Remi and me were growing up; even Katie, when she came to stay, was well behaved. You would have thought Mum would be happy and content with no chewed furniture and not having half the garden dug up and carried indoors, and no mischievous puppy to charge about the house and cause chaos when visitors came but she seemed wistful....I understood her feelings in a way, because it was springtime and it was time for my 'condition'.

Well, you could have knocked me over with a feather when Mum sat me down one day and started talking about the 'birds and the bees'. Poor Mum, I don't think she realised I was a big girl now and, as well as my instincts, I had talked things over with the others and practically seen Remi being born! So when she mentioned about the idea of me having puppies, I was ecstatic.

Mum and Dad discussed things and told me they really, dearly, would love to keep a blue bitch puppy from me. So, shortly, off we went on a long car journey, and I was formerly introduced to Action. He had a long name, but I wasn't bothered or impressed with his having a 'title'. The thing that struck me about him was the twinkle in his eye and...he was devilishly handsome. Of course, it was love at first sight. I fell head-over-hills and....never you mind what the outcome of that was!

On the way home in the car Mum said "Really, Cha Cha, you could have shown a little decorum, been a bit lady-like and played just a teeny bit hard to get! Instead, of throwing yourself at his feet and practically devouring the poor fellow."

Dad commented that he didn't suppose Action minded too much. "What male could fail to be flattered by such utter spontaneity?"

Mum smiled and Dad winked at her. Then she said "I'll cut Cha Cha's coat down shorter tomorrow. She doesn't want to be bothered by oodles of hair when she's got babies to contend with."

"You don't know if she's pregnant yet," Dad said.

"I do. I can tell by the look on her face. And by the way she's making those contented little groans." Dad nodded and smiled. "Keep your eyes and your mind on the road," Mum added.

The girls made a big fuss of me when I got home. They were already excited about the thought of having the patter of little feet running about the place and I promised them they could all have a lick

of the pups once they were here. As it was, I felt frantically protective about my glorious babies for the first ten days. I didn't even want visitors to see them. Mum said it was only natural and anyway the pups were getting a certain amount of early socialisation because we all woke up to Sarah Kennedy on the radio each day. After about a fortnight I was jolly pleased to have the others help with the responsibility of cleaning the kids and keeping them under some sort of control.

Mum picked up each of the pups in turn, every day, and I could see she was having difficulty deciding on which one to keep. Of course, being mine, they were all absolutely lovely.

There was one, naturally, there always is. She kept climbing out of the whelping box and finding her way from the kitchen into the sitting room well before the other pups had given the idea of exploring a thought. Mum didn't realise at the time but this was the one I had chosen for her to keep. In the event, she was down to two pups (one was an angel- as for the other!) When Aunt Jeanne and Uncle Horace from Skegness came to call, Mum held the pups up to show them. "I really love this one, she is so naughty, but this one is an angel...."

Horace looked at me as he caressed each pup in turn. I put my nose on the appropriate one and Mum smiled. "Cha Cha always pokes that pup when I ask her which of the two I should keep."

Horace said "Why argue with the mother?"

The breath left Mum's lungs in a conceding sigh. "It's just that I know Cha Cha and I don't know what I am letting myself in for." I licked her face. And Treasle became part of the family. Poor Mum, bless her.

Until we meet again - **Cha Cha**